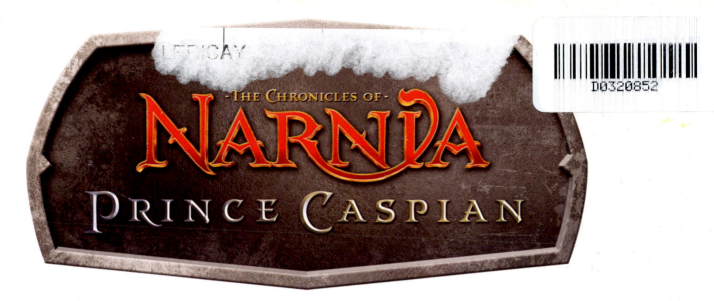

The Tail of Reepicheep

Adapted by E. K. Stein
Illustrated by Justin Sweet
Based on the screenplay by Andrew Adamson & Christopher Markus & Stephen McFeely
Based on the book by C. S. Lewis

Prince Caspian: The Tail of Reepicheep
Copyright © 2008 by C.S. Lewis Pte. Ltd.
Art/illustration © 2008 Disney Enterprises, Inc. and Walden Media, LLC.
Printed in Italy.

This edition published in the United Kingdom in 2008 by HarperCollins Children's Books.
HarperCollins Children's Books is a division of HarperCollins Publishers, 77-85 Fulham Palace Road, Hammersmith, London W6 8JB

www.harpercollinschildrensbooks.co.uk

www.narnia.com

A CIP record for this title is available from the British Library.

978-0-00-725838-3

1 3 5 7 9 10 8 6 4 2

Typography by Rick Farley

PROLOGUE

The land of Narnia is a world filled with amazing creatures. Narnia was once peaceful, but now people called Telmarines have invaded and the evil Miraz is King. Miraz does not want true Narnians in Narnia anymore. For safety, the Narnians hide in the forest.

Legends are told of four children named Peter, Susan, Edmund and Lucy Pevensie. They came to Narnia long ago and the Creator of Narnia, the Great Lion Aslan, crowned them Kings and Queens. They ruled in peace until one day they disappeared.

Not everyone believes these stories. Not everyone believes in Aslan. But some do, including a small but valiant mouse. His name is Reepicheep.

Reepicheep leads an army of twelve other Mice. On his head he wears a gold band with a feather in it to show he is the leader.

Reepicheep and the other Mice in Narnia can talk and are bigger than ordinary mice. They are not as tall as a Dwarf or a Faun, but they are fearsome warriors.

The brave Mice defend the forest, keeping an eye out for Telmarine soldiers.
Reepicheep hears a rustle of leaves and turns to see a Telmarine. The bold Mouse attacks!
Reepicheep waves his small sword in the air.

"Reach for your sword. I will not fight an unarmed man,"
Reepicheep declares.

The Telmarine is a boy. He looks at the fierce Mouse and wisely says,
"I choose not to cross blades with you."

Other Animals come out from behind the trees to see what's happening.

Trufflehunter the Badger knows the boy—his name is Caspian, and he is not an enemy.

Glenstorm the Centaur studies the stars in the sky. The stars say Aslan wants Caspian to be King.

It is decided—Caspian must fight Miraz for the throne.

Even though Reepicheep has never seen Aslan himself, he loves the Great Lion.

Aslan saved Narnia centuries ago, when the evil White Witch ruled the land.

If Aslan wants the boy to be King, then so does Reepicheep.

"If you will lead us, then we will follow you," the Mouse says to Caspian. He salutes.

The Mice are strong fighters, but to battle Miraz and his army, they will need help.
Caspian blows a magical horn that summons the four Kings and Queens from long ago.

It works!

Reepicheep steps forward to greet High King Peter, Queen Susan, King Edmund and Queen Lucy.

"We have awaited your return," Reepicheep says. He hopes that Aslan will return to Narnia, too.

Reepicheep and the Narnians help Caspian and the Pevensie children prepare to fight the Telmarine army. They are ready for battle.

The day arrives. Telmarine soldiers storm the forest on horseback and attack the Narnians. Arrows whistle through the air. Sword clashes against sword.

Reepicheep and his brave Mice use their small size to run along the ground and attack the Telmarines at the ankles. Many Telmarines feel the sting of tiny swords.

Fearing for their lives, the Telmarines retreat across a river. The Mice follow with their swords to the riverbank. When they reach the shore, they can't believe their eyes.

A large Lion stands on the shore. It is Aslan! He has returned to save Narnia!

Aslan commands the river to rise. The raging water washes away the Telmarine army.
Caspian and the Narnians easily defeat the Telmarines left on the shore.

The Narnians have won! Caspian is now King.
Peace will return to Narnia.

Everyone rejoices on the riverbank . . . everyone except the Mice.

A single Mouse marches up to Aslan, playing a sad tune on his pipes.

The other Mice follow, carrying a wounded Reepicheep.

Queen Lucy is able to heal his injuries with a magic cordial.

A moment later, the Mouse rises.

"Hail, Aslan!" cries Reepicheep, but as he bows, he loses his balance.

Looking behind him, Reepicheep sees that his tail is gone! It was lost in battle. He turns back to Aslan in shame.

"A tail is what makes me a Mouse," says Reepicheep sadly.

One Mouse holds a sword to his own tail. He tells Aslan that the other Mice do not want tails if their leader does not have one.

The Lion sees what great hearts the Mice have.

In the blink of an eye, Aslan makes Reepicheep's tail reappear.
The Mice of Narnia rejoice!